Love Unplanned: A Billionaire's Second Chance

When Destiny Intervenes, Billion-Dollar Plans Take a Backseat to Unexpected Love

Emma Nate

© Copyright 2023 - All rights reserved.

The content contained within this book may not be reproduced, duplicated or transmitted without direct written permission from the author or the publisher.

Under no circumstances will any blame or legal responsibility be held against the publisher, or author, for any damages, reparation, or monetary loss due to the information contained within this book, either directly or indirectly.

Legal Notice:

This book is copyright protected. It is only for personal use. You cannot amend, distribute, sell, use, quote or paraphrase any part, or the content within this book, without the consent of the author or publisher.

Disclaimer Notice:

Please note the information contained within this document is for educational and entertainment purposes only. All effort has been executed to present accurate, up to date, reliable, complete information. No warranties of any kind are declared or implied. Readers acknowledge that the author is not engaged in the rendering of legal, financial, medical or professional advice. The content within this book has been derived from various sources. Please consult a licensed professional before attempting any techniques outlined in this book.

By reading this document, the reader agrees that under no circumstances is the author responsible for any losses, direct or indirect, that are incurred as a result of the use of the information contained within this document, including, but not limited to, errors, omissions, or inaccuracies.

Table of Contents

PROLOGUE 1

CHAPTER 1: OLIVIA 3

CHAPTER 2: ETHAN 17

CHAPTER 3: OLIVIA 23

CHAPTER 4: ETHAN 29

CHAPTER 5: OLIVIA 35

CHAPTER 6: ETHAN 39

CHAPTER 7: OLIVIA 43

CHAPTER 8: ETHAN 51

CHAPTER 9: OLIVIA 55

CHAPTER 10: ETHAN 63

Prologue

Doctor Ethan Knight had made quite a name for himself. He was the owner of a billion-dollar company that impacted people's lives in very exponential ways. He revolutionized engineering and got his doctorate because of that. Ethan Knight had become one of the elite businessmen in the world in record time due to his hard work and the fact that no one had ever been brave enough to say no to him for any reason.

Olivia Turner has always been a quiet and shy girl. She hated confrontation and making waves. Olivia only lived to please her parents and make a difference in the world. The only way she could think of how to do that was to become an engineer. Now, in her final semester of college, Olivia needs to start tackling the true nuances of adulting.

Chapter 1:

Olivia

Olivia stood in front of the bathroom mirror, frowning at her appearance. Next to her, her best friend, Keren, was busy applying a thick line of black eyeliner. She had done all of her other makeup, and was dressed in a metal top and white washed jeans.

"What's wrong?" Keren asked, her golden brown eyes meeting Olivia's grey ones in the mirror.

"I just...I'm not feeling the hair." Olivia sighs. She ran her fingertips through the light brown waves that reached her collarbones. Keren had lovely dark brown hair that always looked like it was given a fresh blowout.

"Straighten it." Keren suggests.

Olivia hummed. She wasn't sure if that would make a difference.

"Just leave it how it is. You won't need to feel it the moment we're at the club." Jaylinn said, entering the bathroom. Jaylinn was dressed in a tight fitted black dress with cutouts that showed off her curves. Her thick black hair was slicked back into a high ponytail.

Olivia frowned. She didn't actually want to go to the club. Her roommates had decided that going clubbing for Keren's birthday was a very good idea. Olivia hated clubbing.

"How would you like to wear your hair, Liv?" Elise asked, trailing in behind Jaylinn. Elise was dressed in a beige dress with small sparkles on. Her blonde hair was curled neatly down her back.

Olivia sighed. "It doesn't matter. I'll just go like this."

Olivia felt uncomfortable in the tight fitted white silk dress that had a slit all the way up to her hip.

Keren was the tomboy of the group, and also the party animal. Since it was her 24th birthday, the girls had decided to go out, much to Olivia's disdain.

Jaylinn was the original mastermind behind the idea for Keren's birthday. Jaylinn always took charge in the group.

Elise was the peace keeper, and the one you could always go to when you needed a shoulder to cry on.

Keren sent a wink to Olivia through the mirror. "I appreciate that you're willing to come along, despite your aversion to crowds."

Olivia gave Keren a small warm smile.

"We'll stick together, yeah? We'll have fun as long as we don't get separated." Elise offered, trying very hard to be supportive and helpful.

***

The flashing lights were immediately starting to give Olivia a headache the moment she walked into the club. The pounding bass if the music reverberated through her skull and made her teeth rattle in her jaw. She could smell the sweat and alcohol that was spilled on the floor. Olivia felt out of place.

"Come on, Liv! You need to loosen up!" Jaylinn shouted over the music slinging her arm over Olivia's shoulder and leading her to the bar.

"I'm going to buy you a drink so you can chill out!" Jaylinn shouted over the music, speaking close to Olivia's ear so that she could hear her.

Before Olivia could protest, Jaylinn turned back to the bar, and turned around with two colorful drinks in pretty glasses. She handed one to Olivia, who eyed it suspiciously.

"This thing should get you fucked up quickly." Jaylinn said, grabbing Olivia's free hand and leading her back over to the table where Keren and Elise had found themselves.

"This is so awesome, the music here is really good." Keren shouted. Olivia sipped at her drink, hoping that she wouldn't be too conscious for the rest of the night.

***

Jaylinn had been partially right about the drink. It tasted like a fruit salad, but didn't make Olivia as drunk as Jaylinn said it would.

But it did give Olivia the buzz she needed to be able to let lose a little bit.

Olivia was swaying her hips on the dance floor with Keren and Jaylinn who were both busting it down to the bass line of the song. Elise was over at the bar talking to a guy who was buying her a drink.

Olivia's skin prickled when she felt a pair of eyes on her. She turned her head to the side to see who it was.

A handsome man was watching her from the VIP section on the floor above. He had well kept black curly hair and a handsome face. His skin was pale and extremely smooth. He was dressed in a black button up, with his sleeves rolled up to his elbows, and dark blue jeans. He was leaning forward slightly, watching her dance. Somehow his gaze made Olivia more confident.

She started swaying more with the music, not breaking eye contact with the man. She even raised her arms above her head, starting to feel the music move through her.

Olivia forgot about all of the people, the loud music, the terrible smells. All she was aware of was the beautiful man, and his beautiful eyes, and his razor sharp focus on her.

The man got to his feet. Olivia's breath hitched. He looked tall, and he was broad shouldered. He started walking towards the stairs of the VIP section.

It was as if this man was a magnet. The closer he came to her, the closer she was drawn to him.

She met him at the edge of the dance floor.

"Hi." The man said. His voice was magnificent. It reminded Olivia of the sound of waves breaking.

"Hi." Olivia breathed.

"Would you like to dance?" The man asked, holding his hand out to her. Olivia felt as if her brain wasn't working well.

"One dance, then we get to talk." Olivia said.

The man smiled. He had gorgeous dimples.

"That sounds perfect."

Olivia was surprised when he took her in his arms, and started swaying with her. She had half expected him to start grinding behind her.

The affectionate and gentlemanly action had caught her off guard, and caused her to turn beet red.

The man was warm, and smelt of a very expensive cologne. There was a strong hint of sage, maybe some sandalwood. He was warm, too. But not in a stifling way, more in a comforting way.

Up close, this man was even more gorgeous. He had thick dark brows and magnificent green eyes that were framed with dark lashes. His eyes were intense, but had a youthful quality to them. He had a strong but chiseled nose, and beautiful lips. His cheekbones and jaw were somehow in perfect balance. He was glorious to look at.

The song was over before she would have liked it to be.

"Now, we talk." The man said, his voice soft and inviting. Olivia found herself nodding, and letting herself be led off of the dance floor and up the stairs to the VIP section by the gorgeous man.

He led her over to a table, and she took a seat. The man sat down next to her. Olivia had no idea how to talk to this man, he was that gorgeous.

"What's your name?" The man asked, leaning forward so that he could hear her better. It was much quieter here in the VIP section.

"Olivia." Olivia breathed. This man made her feel light headed and weak in the knees. It was terrifying and exhilarating at the exact same time.

The man smiled. "What a beautiful name. My name is Ethan."

"Ethan." Olivia repeated back to him.

Ethan smiled. "How old are you?"

"I'm twenty-two." Olivia answered. Her brain felt mushy around this man. "And you?"

"I'm twenty-eight."

Olivia felt herself nodding. This man was so gorgeous, it made her social skills non-existent.

A waiter came over to the table, and Ethan ordered two Cokes.

"Normally if people buy me drinks, it's to try and get me drunk." Olivia quipped.

"Why would I want you drunk, when I can enjoy a sober conversation with you?"

Ethan was a breed of man that Olivia had never encountered before. He was kind and confident. She wanted to drink it all in.

***

"Let's take this back to my place." Ethan said after two rounds of Coke.

"It's my friend's birthday-" Olivia begins, but stops herself quickly. She'll send them a text in the group chat. They would understand. "Yeah, we can go back to yours."

***

Ethan pressed Olivia against the hard wood of his bedroom door, his body completely covering hers. His hand wrapped around her throat, titling her head up. His thumb grazed along the side of her jugular, his digits pressing into the supple skin of her neck.

Olivia was on fire. Ethan's touch on her neck was electric. His other hand was on her hip, pressing her against the door, every line and contours of his body pressed against hers.

His eyes were magnificent. His lips were on hers. His lips were warm, but it was clear that he knew what he was doing. His tongue was in her mouth, tasting her, exploring her. He knew too much, and it was tantalizing.

Ethan was an experience, and he knew it.

Her nails dug into the wood of the door, desperate.

"You know you can touch me, right?" Ethan asked breaking the kiss, his smile dazzling nd leaving Olivia dazed.

Olivia swallowed hard, and Ethan moved his lips down her neck. His kisses were self-assured, warm and wet on her neck. Olivia's hands shook as she moved them up to hold onto his shoulder and forearm.

Ethan nipped at her neck, and Olivia gasped. She was putty in this man's hands. They both knew it, and as terrifying as it was, it was liberating.

His hand that was on her hip was momentarily gone, and then the door behind her gave way. Olivia clung to

Ethan tightly so that she wouldn't fall. She felt him chuckle against her neck. He did that on purpose.

His one hand traced down her back, over her ass and to the groove where her ass and thigh met. He lifted her up, making her wrap her leg around his waist. His lips were on her again in another dizzying kiss.

Her back met the soft sheets of Ethan's bed. They were a warm cotton, soft to the touch, but very high quality.

Ethan had kicked off his shoes at the door, and Olivia reached to unclasp her heels.

Ethan's warm hand stopped her, caressing her ankle. "Leave the shoes on."

Olivia blinked in confusion, but widened her eyes when Ethan started unbuttoning his black shirt. His skin was still perfectly pale, but his muscular form was quite spectacular to stare at.

Ethan placed his hands on her hips, lifting up the silk of her dress. Olivia could feel her face heat at Ethan's piecing gaze that hadn't left her face.

"Has anyone ever told you that you are a work of art?" Ethan asked, his voice thick and warm.

Olivia could feel her self turn even redder, if that was possible. "No." She squeaked.

"Then let me be the first to admire you as art should be admired." Ethan said, kneeing down at the foot of the bed.

Olivia sat up slightly, not expecting to see Ethan pulling her underwear down her legs.

"Wh-what are you doing?" Olivia asked, sounding like she was already gasping for breath. It was a sight that would knock the wind out of anyone, a man like Ethan between her thighs.

Ethan grinned up at her, his gorgeous hands trailing over her thighs. "Admiring the art."

His mouth was on her, and Olivia yelped. His tongue was warm and wet and oh so skilled, going into all the right crevices and stroking all the right places.

She let out a guttural moan, her hands moving to cling to Ethan's curly hair. She felt him grin against her and nip at her.

Olivia couldn't contain the sound he was pulling from her, and the wet noises that his tongue made on her were lewd, but so delicious.

A knot was tying itself in her stomach, building, building.

The precipice of the feeling that crashed over her had her hips gyrating against Ethan's face. His forearm shoved her hips down, protecting his face in case she bucked too sharply.

Ethan continued his assault on her most sensitive parts, demanding another release from her.

The focus on Ethan's face and the intensity in his eyes made that knot snap again in her stomach.

"Please, please give me something more." Olivia begged.

Ethan lifted his head, smirking at her. "Are you tired of being admired?"

"Yes, now I want to be fucked." Olivia whined, half surprised by her own statement.

Ethan grinned, getting to his feet. "All right, your wish is my command."

She got the delectable view of Ethan unzipping his jeans and pulling down his Calvin Klein boxer briefs.

His dick stood at attention, pale, long and girthy. The sight of it made Olivia start to salivate.

"Ass up for me." Ethan said, hooking his arm underneath Olivia's knee and flipping her over, so that her chest was pressed to the bed.

His hands delicately traced the zipper on the back of her dress, freeing her skin from the silky material.

Olivia freed her arms from the spaghetti straps, and Ethan pulled the dress down and off of her body.

She wished she could look back at him, to see his eyes again and to see what he was thinking.

All thoughts were forgotten the moment he pressed into her. She could feel every delectable inch of him, and his warm hands on her hips pulled her back against him.

"So perfect." Ethan hissed through his teeth, moving her hips and his in tandem, meeting in the middle.

The sounds and sensations Ethan was drawing from Olivia should have been criminal. She could never even draw them from herself with her own vibrator.

Ethan started picking up the speed, his hands moving to claw at her waist to support his speed. Olivia dropped her chest to the bed, groaning at the new angle that was reached. Every time her and Ethan's hips met, she ground back on him, never wanting the sensation to stop.

He was good, able to reach parts in her her fingers had never even explored. He was hitting all the right places, as if his dick was made to pleasure her the moment it entered her, a perfect fit.

Olivia crumbled under Ethan, her third orgasm overtaking her. The moment Ethan felt her clench around him, he picked up his pace, now no longer caring if she got any pleasure out of his movements, chasing his own release.

His hands dung into the flesh of her ass, pulling and pushing her on his dick, while still keeping his brutal jackhammering pace. The sensation had Olivia screaming and clawing at the sheets, her walls raw and over sensitive to every ridge on him.

Olivia clenched a fourth time, this time around nothing, as Ethan pulled out, spilling his warm seed onto her back and ass cheeks. Ethan came with a deep guttural groan.

"Look at you, so pretty and perfect when you're fucked out." Ethan panted, using his finger to trace what felt like a signature on her back in his cum.

Chapter 2:

Ethan

Ethan glanced over the content for his university lecture once more, making sure he had the content down. He had all of his papers spread out across his desk, and a few notes scribbled down of what he needed to cover in that day's class.

This wasn't the first lecture he'd ever given, no. But this would be his first full semester he had to lecture for, every day at eight in the morning.

His friend, Francois, the Dean of the university had called in the favor when they were playing golf together a month ago. The previous lecturer had mysteriously quit, and Francois needed to temporarily fill the opening till he could employ someone permanently.

"And since you have doctorate in engineering, it should be a piece of cake for you." Francois had said, swinging his golf club.

Ethan's attention snapped to the door as the first students started trickling into the lecture hall, some fast asleep and others too focused on their phones to notice him. But those that did notice him seemed to be struck by lightning the moment they recognized him. How could they not? He was the owner of Knight industries, after all.

And then she walked in.

That girl that danced like nothing in the world mattered. The girl that was free as a bird, and beautiful as a sunset.

Olivia.

What the hell was she doing in his class?

He completely forgot to ask her what she does for a living. How could he have been so stupid?

Ethan's face heated remembering Friday night. He had literally signed his name in his cum on her back, and now he had to teach a class with her in.

What now? He couldn't just leave. He had promised Francois he'd do it.

Ethan watched Olivia walk to the middle of the class, not having noticed him yet, since she was busy talking to a blonde girl that she walked in with. Olivia was dressed in jeans and a sweatshirt, a stark contrast to that beautiful dress she wore on Friday night.

The last few students trickled in, and Ethan turned away from the class, looking at the board. He put his hands on his hips. How could his luck be so terrible?

Ethan took a steeling breath, before turning around to face the class. A yelp came from somewhere in the class. Ethan plastered his best grin on his face.

"Welcome to you final semester of Mechatronics. I'll be your professor for this semester. My name is Doctor Ethan Knight. I'm also the owner and founder of Knight enterprise, before you ask."

Ethan's eyes trailed over the faces who immediately started whispering. Olivia was staring squarely at her desk, looking at her light blue binder like it was the most fascinating thing in the world.

Like hell, he was far more interesting to look at than a binder. Ethan didn't know why, but her not looking at him while he was speaking irked him. He decided to let it slide, and see if it continues.

***

After a week of class with either Olivia skipping or refusing to look at him, Ethan's irritation with her was through the roof. Was she embarrassed of their time together? Ethan's ego wouldn't allow for that to be the case. He would make her look at him, somehow.

He pretends to read off of the attendance list to get names. He picked a name so that it would seem random.

"Mathew...Parker. What is the answer to question four on the board?"

A kid with thick black glasses rattled off the answer, Ethan only listening with half an ear. "Yeah, great. Well done."

He scanned the list again, deciding he would ask Olivia. It was one way to get her to look at him.

"Olivia Turner, you should know this from your first year. What is mechatronics?"

Olivia's head snapped up to look at him. Ethan couldn't stop the grin that spread across his face. Yes, Olivia looked positively pissed off, but at least she was looking at him.

"Sir, with all due respect, that is not in our current syllabus." Olivia answered. She seemed positively peeved.

"I don't care. What is the definition of mechatronics?" Ethan repeated, unable to wipe the shit eating grin off of his face at Olivia's red face and annoyance.

"Well, *sir*, mechatronics is a branch in engineering that combined electrical and mechanical engineering." Olivia said, her tone sarcastic. Ethan wouldn't have that tone.

"That's a terrible definition, but that's to be expected from someone who doesn't seem to pay attention in the class." Ethan quipped. The class snickered at her expense.

Ethan wasn't sure why he was so set on having Olivia's eyes on him, but he really enjoyed the attention she gave him. It made him feel more confident in what he was doing.

Olivia glared down bashfully at her desk. "Look at me when I am speaking, or take notes, whatever you prefer.

But pay attention to what I say." Ethan said, glancing over all of the faces staring at him. His eyes trailed back over to Olivia. She glared down at her notebook and clicked her pen, before fixing her steely gaze on him, enraged.

Ethan grinned. "Great, let's continue."

Chapter 3:

Olivia

Olivia was fuming. Ethan was such an ass! He called her out in front of the whole class. First of all, how dare he? Second of all, why did he insist on making her look at him?

Olivia marched into the Dean's office, visibly peeved and annoyed.

The Dean looked up when she entered. "Good morning, to what do I owe your impertinence?"

Olivia was red in the face, and her fists were balled at her sides. "Sir, how do I swap lecturers? My current professor and I don't see *eye to eye*." Olivia spat.

The Dean sighed. "Go to academics-"

"I want it done now. And for that to happen, I need your seal of approval. So I am asking you directly."

The Dean raised an eyebrow, but clicked around on his computer.

"Faculty?"

"Engineering." Olivia answered. She couldn't believe the audacity of Ethan. He made her look like an idiot, when she was obviously smarter than everyone else in the room.

The Dean typed on his computer. "Semester?"

"Final."

The Dean clicked around.

"Specialization?"

"Mechatronics." Olivia answered. She needed to move. Ethan was unfair in class. He'll probably be unfair again in her tests, and she couldn't have that.

"Name?"

"Olivia Turner." Olivia answered.

"Course you wish to drop?"

"Mechatronics."

The Dean snorted. "That's a mandatory class for your degree. You can't drop it. Sorry."

He didn't sound very sorry.

"Can I transfer?" Olivia seethed.

"No, we only have Professor Knight." The Dean said. "What happened that has you so upset?"

Olivia debated telling him all about how she and Ethan met, but refrained. That will make her look bad.

"He is rude, and I'm worried he won't be fair in tests." Olivia answered instead.

The Dean laughed. "Who, Ethan? No, he's the most fair guy I knw. He's very objective, too. He won't mark you down unless you fail."

Olivia frowned. This will get her no where.

***

"And then he told me that Ethan is like...super fair!" Olivia ranted. She and Keren were walking back to their apartment after class. The had stopped and gotten an emotional support coffee for Olivia that needs to go sit and study for her semester test coming up.

"So you didn't tell the dean that you want to move due to your sex-capades with your professor?" Keren asked, sipping her latte.

"Of course not! Shit like that goes on your record, like...permanently!" Olivia ranted.

"Ouch. In the art department we're all anyway sleeping with each other, so no one really cares." Keren mused.

"Your degree is about self-expression. Mine is about clear cut rules. And now I feel like the lines will be blurred. He'll fail me to get me out of his class. He clearly doesn't want me there. I'm going to fail, and then what?" Olivia asked. Her voice was full of melancholy.

"Then you become a stripper. Easy." Keren snorted.

***

Olivia sat in class, barely able to keep her eyes open as she's writing the semester test. She had pulled an all-nighter and was exhausted. She had a Redbull and three coffees in, but that didn't help her tired state. To top it all off, she also had a headache.

She may be coming down with something, given her flushed and feverish feeling too.

Olivia's eyes drifted closed.

***

Olivia inhaled sharply. Her back was terribly sore. She sat up with a start.

The lecture hall was completely empty, save for Ethan, who was leaning on the desk in front of her.

"Wake up, sleeping beauty. Your test is three hours overdue." Ethan said.

Olivia looked up at him. He was dressed in a grey sweater and black slacks. He looked formal, but surprisingly approachable. He smelt of that expensive cologne with strong hints of sage.

"What? Did I fail the test?" Olivia asked.

"Unfortunately, yes, since you didn't hand in at the stipulated time." Ethan answered.

Olivia could feel her face heating in rage.

"It's because of you that I didn't sleep!" Olivia accused.

Chapter 4:

Ethan

"I didn't think I made such an impression, princess." Ethan quipped, his mouth pulling into a slight smirk.

Olivia was so shocked by Ethan's comment that she needed a moment to recover.

"It's because you can't be professional with me! I knew you'd fail me unless I could get nothing wrong!" Olivia accused.

Ethan frowned. "Where'd you get that idea? Olivia, I've been nothing but professional. I would have given you a fair grade, regardless of any external factors."

Olivia scoffed. "Yeah, right. You humiliated me in front of the class!"

Ethan tried to remember what instance she was talking about.

Olivia scoffed at his lack of response.

"That wasn't me humiliating you. That was me trying to get you to pay attention, so that this could have been avoided." Ethan said, gesturing to Olivia who was still seated.

Olivia scoffed. "So this is my fault?"

"Well, yes. Choices have consequences. If you paid attention in my class you would have known all the content well enough to get more than a passing grade." Ethan answered.

Olivia huffed, annoyed.

"Why don't you focus in my class?" Ethan asked after a moment. He wanted to help Olivia succeed, for some or other inexplicable reason. He'd delude himself later into believing he'd care enough about all of the students to try to get them to succeed.

"I can't." Olivia said firmly. Ethan raised an eyebrow in disbelief.

"And why is that?"

Ethan could see the defiance behind her eyes when she looked at him. He steeled his gaze, starring her down. He watched her resolve crumble like fresh snow.

"You are too distracting." Olivia said after a beat of silence.

Ethan grinned, raising an eyebrow. "Really?"

Olivia sighed in frustration, getting up from her desk. She moved to walk around him, and he let her.

Olivia started for the door, but Ethan stopped at his desk.

"Olivia."

Olivia turned, very annoyed by the interaction.

"I try to be distracting."

Olivia's jaw hung open.

"Come put your mouth to good use." Ethan said.

Ethan hadn't expected Olivia to actually come over to him. Olivia's bright grey eyes were wide and innocent as she looked at him. "How would you like me?"

Ethan moved behind his desk, sitting down on his chair. "On your knees for me."

Olivia's immediate obedience was startling. When she sat on her knees in front of Ethan, the semi-hard on he had been nursing all day sprung to attention and twitched painfully. Her hands were on his belt, her eyes looking up at him, watching his face for any reaction.

Ethan sat back, waiting to see how far she'd take this. Olivia was in no mood to give up, as was evident when her hands unzipped his fly, and she moved his clothes aside so that his dick sprung free.

He was yet again impressed by his own size. His dick was as long as her face, and Olivia watching Olivia's eyes widen was satisfaction enough.

"Backing out now, princess?" Ethan taunted.

"Never." Olivia said, glaring up at him. Olivia took his dick in both of her hands, forcing the tip into her mouth.

Ethan hissed. She ran her tongue over the slit, and tongued around the tip. Ethan instinctively wrapped a hand in her hair. He was fighting every urge he had not to buck his hips. Olivia was good, too good at this.

Olivia took more and more of him in her mouth with each bob of her head. He loved the teary look in her eyes and his dick in her mouth.

"Fuck, you're perfect." Ethan hissed through his teeth. Olivia seemed to need to prove a point, and licked a long stripe up his shaft from base to tip.

"Nope, get up." Ethan said, yanking Olivia up to her feet. Ethan stood up, and a string of saliva connected his dick and her plump lips.

"Did I do something wrong?" Olivia asked innocently. Ethan put his hands on her hips, backing her into his desk.

"You're doing too well. You know too much. I don't want to think about why." Ethan said. "Get on the desk. Panties at your knees, skirt up."

Olivia had a cheeky grin on her face, flipping up her skirt. Ethan noticed that she was wearing a cute lacey thong. She hooked her thumb into the side of her panties, pulling it down to her knees and hopped onto the desk.

Ethan couldn't help his eyes roaming her now exposed cunt. It was so pretty. But he needed her under him, now.

Ethan wrapped a hand around her neck, shoving her back down onto the desk, hard. Olivia made a surprised noise, but swallowed it when Ethan took both of her knees and put them over his left shoulder.

Ethan's grip on her neck tightened as he slipped into her, a groan leaving his lips. This position made her impossibly tight. A moan rolled off of her tongue, and if Ethan could he's bottle the sound and get drunk on it every night.

The first roll of his hips was slow, gentle even. But then Ethan remembered why he wanted her in this position. He wanted to remind her who the fuck he was.

Ethan started pounding into Olivia at a brutal pace, one that made her gasp and choke out screams at each thrust.

The sound that his dick made in her was devastatingly delicious. He was ruining her in a way that was a slow but delectable torture. He'd give her the best, and ruin her average sex she'd ever have with anyone else ever again.

He was surprised by Olivia's sob that escaped her. But he couldn't deny the sick twitch in his dick at the way the tears were rolling down her face.

"Ah, Ethan." Olivia sobbed. "I can't."

"You can and you will." Ethan said firmly. He was thrusting so fast and so hard and so deep that Olivia was being dragged across the desk by his dick inside of her.

Ethan didn't think it was humanly possible for her to get any tighter due to the position, but she clenched so hard he was immediately squeezed into an orgasm. The contraction at the base of his spine was harder than he expected it to be, and he could feel her milking him dry as his hot spurts filled her.

Chapter 5:

Olivia

Olivia's excitement to go to her mechatronics class was new. Maybe it was due to the fact that she hoped Ethan would fuck her again after class. She felt him all of yesterday, and when she sat down at her desk to study the night before she clenched at the memory of him. To be able to focus, she had to get herself off at her desk. It would be a perfect time for Ethan to rail her again, as Elise was sick back at the apartment, so she could stay as long as she needed to.

A friend of Olivia's from her second year falls into step beside her. It was William Nelson. He had curly blond hair and striking blue eyes. He was conventionally attractive, but he wasn't Olivia's type because he was too much of a Golden Retriever type.

"Hey, Liv. Can I sit with you, since Elise isn't here?" William asked. She hated that he called her that.

"Sure. But I need to focus in class, so no talking please." Olivia asked, offering a kind smile to soften the blow.

William nodded, but started babbling immediately. Olivia suppressed an eyeroll and walked into class, William trailing behind.

Ethan was looking delicious enough to take a bite out of. He was dressed in a pressed white t-shirt and a pair of really well fitting blue jeans. He had a brown suit jacket on over the t-shirt. Olivia hoped her floral sundress would be enough of an attention grabber. As she walked up the stairs to her seat, she could feel multiple pairs of eyes on her ass. She glanced behind her, and she noticed the light dusting of pink on William's face.

Olivia took her seat, listening with half an ear to William's discussion he was having with himself.

"Good morning." Ethan said.

"-but I think that-" William continued.

Ethan's piercing gaze snapped over to William sitting next to Olivia.

"Mister Nelson. I'd like to start my lesson." Ethan said. Olivia could tell his patience was razor thin today.

William shut up immediately, looking down at his desk.

"As you all know, in your final semester, you have three tests and a big assignment. You've already written one of your tests. The assignment-"

"Do you want to be partners?" William asked.

Before Olivia could respond. "Nelson, shut it. I'm busy explaining seventy-percent of your grade. I'd suggest you listen." Ethan said.

William turned back to look at Ethan again.

"This is an individual assignment. So no partners. We will be going to the San Francisco bridge for the project. Your job, will be to take notes and then build a model and give a presentation on how you would have built the bridge." Ethan explained.

"Yay, roadtrip. I know it's an individual assignment, but we can still work together-" William started.

"Nelson. Get out. You fail." Ethan said simply.

"What! No-you can't do that-" William tried to protest.

"Yes, I can. Because I have the doctorate. And in the student code of conduct, you mustn't speak in class unless the floor is open to do so. So get out."

Olivia couldn't help the wet spot that she could feel forming on her chair. Ethan spoke with such authority. She hoped she could get him to speak like that to her soon.

William stared in disbelief, but started packing up his stuff. Ethan stared him down as he kept explaining.

"As an incentive, the student who gets the top score will have a job at my firm the day you graduate." Ethan said. His eyes followed William until he was on his way out of the door. Ethan's eyes snapped back over to Olivia. She couldn't help the blush that was forming on her face.

Chapter 6:

Ethan

Ethan sat at a table in a bar across from his latest potential business partner, Mumbai Steel. If he could close this business deal, he would never have to worry about factoring steel costs into any of his projects ever again.

"There is just one problem, however." Amir, the figurehead of Mumbai Steel said. "We did some reading on you. Your wife, she is here?"

Ethan paled. He hadn't gone public with his divorce from Lize three years ago.

"No, my ex-wife and I aren't currently on speaking terms." Ethan answered.

Amir frowned. "Oh, I thought you had a wife."

Ethan could tell this was going sour. "No, I have a fiancée. She's lovely."

Amir seemed to perk up at the mention of a fiancée. "Oh, lovely. We can go through with the deal the moment I meet her."

Ethan panicked. His eyes trailed across the room for who he could ask quickly, and his eyes landed on Olivia.

"Oh, all right. She's here with some friends, waiting for me to finish up. I'll go get her quickly." Ethan said, excusing himself.

He walked over to the table where Olivia was sitting with her friends.

"Olivia, I need your help. Now." Ethan speaks. Olivia eyes him suspiciously.

"Why?" Olivia asked, swirling around her drink in her glass and sipping it through the thin straw.

"Get a ring. I will buy you a new car if you help me." Ethan asked. He wouldn't resort to begging. Olivia was a bit of an ass in front of her friends to him. He wondered if they knew how easily she submits the moment she is alone.

Olivia turned to one of her friends, holding out her hand. The girl took off a hug sparkly ring and put it in Olivia's waiting palm.

Olivia hooked in arms with Ethan, slipping the ring onto her finger. "So what needs to happen?"

"I need you to be my fiancée to close a business deal." Ethan murmured. "Look absolutely enamored with me."

Ethan was impressed by the besotted look she managed to paste on her face.

Amir smiled broadly when he saw Ethan approach with Olivia on his arm.

"Oh, is this the lovely lady? You must have a lovely name, no?" Amir asked, taking Olivia's hand to shake.

Ethan felt his skin prickle at Amir's flirtatious tone.

"Olivia Turner." Olivia said with a dazzling smile. Ethan wanted to scowl. He didn't like how Amir seemed to suddenly only be interested in talking to Olivia. How dare he speak to her in such a manner.

"I'm so sorry, Amir. But I promised the love of my life we could leave soon, so I shall be taking her home now." Ethan interjected.

"Ethan, I do not mean to arouse any jealousy. She is just so lovely, I cannot believe you haven't shown off this beautiful gem." Amir laughed, raising his hands in defense.

Ethan narrowed his eyes, but smiled and shook Amir's hand before dragging Olivia to the door.

Chapter 7:

Olivia

Olivia woke up to a tabloid article with a photo of her and Ethan on the cover, the ring that she borrowed from Keren on full display as they left the bar. She had no idea when that photo was even taken. She hadn't seen a flash go off or nothing.

Elise burst into Olivia's room, the very article Olivia was reading moments before on full display on her screen.

"What the fuck are we going to do if your parents see this?"

Olivia paled. She never thought about that. "The Dean? Our classmates?" Elise continued to list off.

"What can I do?" Olivia groaned. "I can't tell anyone its fake. Then the news will get out, and I promised I wouldn't."

"Well, this is a mess." Elise mused.

***

After a long bus ride and the visit to the bridge later, Olivia was ready to go to her hotel room and relax before they had to leave again the next morning.

"What do you mean there was a misunderstanding?" Ethan asked the little man at the front desk who cowered away at his tone.

"I'm sorry-we thought because you're engaged you wouldn't mind sharing-" The little man squeaked out.

Olivia groaned in disbelief, walking over to Ethan who was about to grab the little man.

"It's fine. We can make a plan." Olivia sighed out.

The receptionist sent her a relieved look. "Thank you, miss, for your understanding-"

"You don't get to talk to her after your incompetence." Ethan hissed, taking the room keys and walking towards the elevator.

Olivia jogged to keep up, stepping into the elevator behind him.

"What's up your ass that's got you so upset?" Olivia asked in a dry tone.

Ethan sighed in frustration. "I'm sorry, I didn't think our arrangement would have such a big impact. I'm usually very good at catching the tabloids."

Olivia gave Ethan a tight-lipped smile. "It happens. Now we just need to make the best out of a bad situation."

"I'll sleep on the floor." Ethan replied.

Olivia rolled her eyes. "We're both adults. We'll be fine."

***

Laying in bed next to Ethan made her realize this would not be fine.

Ethan smelled divine, and she could feel his arm touching hers due to the surprisingly small bed.

Olivia did what she always did when she was panicking, she started talking.

"So...why did you need me to pose as you fiancée for that business meeting?"

Ethan sighed deeply, as if he didn't really want to talk about it, but he knew he should. "Mumbai Steel is a family run company. They exclusively want to do business with people who are also family orientated. And because I don't have any family, I needed to improvise."

"What do you mean you don't have any family?" Olivia asked quietly.

"I was in the foster care system till I turned seventeen, so I never had any family. And my wife divorced me." Ethan explained.

"What? But you're only twenty-eight?" Olivia frowned.

"We met in college, and due to my living arrangements, the fact that Lize had an apartment was a huge motivating factor, so we got married at eighteen."

"Why did you get divorced?" Olivia asked.

Olivia turned to look over at Ethan. He seemed to be debating with himself if he was goin to tell her.

"Lize's dad gave me the money to start the company, in exchange that I marry her. The company paid for my studies. And then Lize cheated on me, multiple times with multiple people. And I decided I was done. I bought her dad out of the company and divorced her."

"That's...I never knew that." Olivia murmured.

"So, with that in mind, just know I have no interest in really being married. But Amir sent an email, saying that if I don't get married, there is no deal."

Olivia remained silent.

"So we can work something out-"

Olivia grinned, turning on her side to face Ethan.

"If you wanted easy access to me, all you had to do was ask."

"I don't need easy access. I already have it." Ethan murmured darkly.

In the darkness of the room, she didn't see Ethan's hand move until it was on the inside of her thigh.

Olivia gasped, and Ethan chuckled, looking at her. His hand slid all the way to her core, cupping it.

"See? Easy access?" Ethan hummed, beginning to thumb her clit through her underwear and pajama shorts.

Olivia made a high-pitched sound in response. Ethan moved her shorts and panties to the side, his thumb still thumbing her clit, but slipping four fingers inside of her.

Olivia gasped in surprise at the intrusion, but Ethan's lips were on her neck. Her thoughts melted away, and all she could think of was Ethan, and how delicious his fingers felt.

"Ethan." Olivia gasped.

Ethan withdrew his hand, rolling on top of Olivia, planting a wet kiss on her lips.

Ethan pulled down his pajama bottoms slightly, freeing himself and giving himself a few pumps.

Olivia almost drooled at the sight of him.

Ethan pushed her panties and pajama shorts to the side, entering her swiftly.

His dick felt so good. No matter how many times he was in her, he never managed to lose the appeal to her of having him in her again.

Olivia du her nails into his biceps, reveling in the feeling of Ethan' dick scraping against her walls.

Olivia let her head lull to the side, but Ethan used his finger to turn her head back. "No. Eyes on me."

Olivia gasped at his words.

Ethan reached his hand down between their bodies again, rubbing her clit furiously. Olivia gasped, dragging her hips up with Ethan's.

Ethan kissed her furiously, any sounds she made being swallowed by him.

Olivia felt herself tighten around him, falling over the precipice that he was drawing her to. Ethan fell over the precipice just after her, wrapping his arms around her, holding her close like he was afraid of losing her.

Olivia returned the tight embrace. Ethan buried his face in her neck, sighing deeply.

"Give me time to get a dress for our elopement." Olivia breathed.

"Okay." Ethan murmured. He was falling asleep.

It occurred to Olivia that she had never seen Ethan sleep.

Her mother told her that a man that falls asleep after sex feels safe with you. Olivia grinned when she heard the gentle snores coming from Ethan, while he was still snuggled on her, buried to the hilt inside her.

***

Olivia woke up to an empty hotel room. Ethan's things were all still standing around. A coffee cup that he had gotten from Starbucks stood on his bedside table with a note attached.

Gone to the gym, be back soon beautiful

E

Olivia grinned at the note, and reached for the coffee, sipping the latte Ethan had guessed perfectly.

Chapter 8:

Ethan

Ethan sat in his large leather chair in his office. It had been two weeks since the San Francisco trip. He and Olivia were eloping this afternoon. She had gone out with his credit card and bought herself a pretty dress, and he couldn't wait to see it.

Being with Olivia, even if he wasn't with her, was easier.

She was easy to talk to. For some or other reason, he felt like he could talk to her, and that she'd listen to him.

And they worked very well together in the bedroom.

Despite their arrangement, Ethan was looking forward to being married to Olivia.

***

Ethan's breath hitched when he saw Olivia. She was dressed in a pretty pale yellow dress that was made of a silky material and was off the shoulder. It may have been a simple sundress, but he thought she looked magnificent.

Her three roommates trailed behind her, each in a black dress with veiled hats.

"What's with the get up?" Ethan asked, referring to Olivia's friends.

"We're in mourning, dude. It's the death of one of our favorite bachelorettes." One of Olivia's friends explained dramatically, dabbing at her eyes with a tissue as if she was crying.

They didn't really need to be here, but if Olivia wanted them there, then he's let them be there.

***

When Ethan and Lize had gotten married, it had been a gigantic ceremony with over five hundred people all crowded into a cathedral with impressively high ceilings. He had known no one there besides Lize and her parents. He felt like they were making a spectacle of him, a lamb to a slaughter. The vows were all done in Latin, and he had no idea what he was truly agreeing to.

But this time it was different with Olivia.

As they stood side by side in the clergy's office, repeating the vows that he was reading to them, he felt at peace.

He could appreciate the wave in Olivia's long hair, and the curve of her shoulder, and the line of her arm as she stood next to him. Olivia was truly one of the most beautiful women he had ever seen.

In this moment, he remembered seeing Olivia for the first time. It was like time had slowed. He had spotted her because of her laugh. She was the only person laughing on the dance floor. Everyone else looked like they were searching for something, but Olivia had found it, and she was the treasure and the prize.

Her hair had fanned out around her as she spun around with one of her friends, enthralled by the music. She danced like she never had a care in the world, like she was free as a a bird.

A part of Ethan craved the freedom she seemed to ooze out in that moment. That is why he approached her.

"I do."

The words snapped Ethan back to reality.

"And do you, Ethan Knight, take Olivia Turner to be your lawfully wedded wife?"

The words were out before Ethan even needed to think about them. He knew, deep down, that he was making the right decision. This felt very different to with Lize. This felt right.

"I do."

The clergy nodded. "Sign here and here."

Ethan was disappointed that there was no kiss.

***

"After my exams I'll move my stuff to your place." Olivia said.

Her tone was so formal and business like, it almost made Ethan frown.

"Okay. See you after your exams."

Ethan wasn't sure if he'd be able to wait that long to see her.

Chapter 9:

Olivia

Olivia had spent most of her days for the last two weeks in front of her textbooks at her desk to get as much of the knowledge in her brain.

The only true breaks she was taking was to sleep and write exams.

Keren stopped in her doorway.

"Get dressed, genius. We need to go out." Keren said.

Olivia looked up at her, frowning. "I'm studying."

"You need to get out, or you'll go crazy." Keren said, throwing a shirt at Olivia.

***

Olivia hated clubs. She was yet again reminded of her hatred of large crowds.

Jaylinn was screaming the lyrics of a song in her face, dancing with her drink above her head. Olivia wanted to go home, more than anything.

"Ugh, you're so boring after you got married!" Keren complained.

Olivia spotted Elise talking to someone over at the bar. "I'm going to go get a drink."

"Atta girl!" Keren cheered after her.

"Olivia!" a voice called, and someone grabbed her wrist.

Olivia spun around to face the person, ready to tell them in a very colorful manner that they need to let her go.

Her high school crush, Jackson, stood in front of her. He was captain of the basketball team, and had curly chocolate brown hair. He had a dreamy boyish face.

"Jackson! Hi!" Olivia greeted with a wide smile.

"I wasn't sure it was you, you look so different!" Jackson yelled over the music.

"You look exactly like when we graduated." Olivia laughed.

"Can we go somewhere quitter, to catch up?" Jackson asked.

Olivia glanced at her friends who were busy talking to a group of guys. "Sure."

Jackson led her over to couches just off of the dance floor of the club. The noise didn't really make a difference.

"How are you?" Jackson asked the moment he sat down.

"I'm all right. Did you get the professional contract like you hoped you would?" Olivia asked.

"Oh, no. Not really, anyway. I'm a reserve for the local team-"

This felt like a watered down version of her first meeting with Ethan. Jackson still had to shout due to where they were sitting, which irritated her for some or other reason.

She wondered what Ethan was doing now?

Knowing him, he was marking papers late in his office.

"-but I'll definitely go pro soon. Talent like mine can't be hidden very long, right, so-"

Olivia gave a tight lipped smile as Jackson was talking, nodding along to everything he was saying.

In high school, Olivia would have swooned at him even looking in her direction. He had a committed girlfriend in those days, Chelsea. Chelsea was head of the drama club and a cheerleader. The pairing always made sense.

"-and they said that I have a lot of potential, which is a really good sign-"

Olivia had gone to prom with Jackson, because Chelsea had broken up with him a week before prom. This felt a lot like that night, Jackson talking about himself and his plans.

The only difference was, now, was that she really didn't care. The fact that he was holding a one sided conversation with himself was grating on her nerves.

"-and like the other day at practice, one of my teammates-"

Olivia studied Jackson's face. She now really can't remember what she saw in him in high school. Now, looking at him up close, she was underwhelmed. She had no idea how she could be obsessed with this guy, in hindsight.

Maybe it was the fact that there weren't many other options.

Jackson was leaning forward towards her.

"What are you doing?" Olivia asked.

"Kissing you?" Jackson said, sounding uncertain of himself.

"Why?" Olivia asked, the annoyance in her tone betraying her.

"Because I want to?" Jackson offered.

Before Olivia could reply, Jackson's lips were on hers.

In high school, she would have been thrilled.

Now, she was just disgusted.

It felt like kissing a wet fish. His lips were dead, not doing anything.

Olivia pulled her head back. "Yeah, no. Let's not do that, bud."

Jackson smirked. "Why not? I know you used to have a crush on me in high school."

"Which was four years ago. I'm not the same person I was then, okay?" Olivia said, trying to let him down gently.

"Oh, come on. For old time's sake?" Jackson teased.

Olivia wondered if he thought he was being endearing, or if he was just really stupid.

She held up her left hand with the new ring Ethan had gotten her. "Dude, I'm married, and deeply uninterested in you."

*****

Keren came into Olivia's room at three that following morning, still dressed in her clubbing outfit.

"Liv? Why did you leave?" Keren asked.

Olivia was laying on her bed, her head hanging off of the side.

"I feel like shit." Olivia complained.

Keren smiled sympathetically, coming to sit down next to her and stroking her hair.

"I'm pretty hungover too." Keren commented.

"No, I didn't drink at all, but I feel like I'm going to throw up. And I think I might have a fever. Could it be cholera?" Olivia asked.

Keren groaned. "No, stupid. You could have food poisoning, or an infection of some sort."

Olivia groaned in response, rolling over onto her other side of the bed. Keren flopped down next to her with a sigh.

"Hang on, tell me if I'm tripping...but could you be pregnant?" Keren asked, sitting up suddenly. She groaned and clutched her head at the sudden jarring movement.

"No way. I would know, right? Mother's intuition and all of that bs? It's probably just exam stress." Olivia reasoned.

"Don't be a dumbass." Keren scolded. "Pee on a stick. Better safe than sorry."

***

Olivia and Keren waited for the pregnancy test's timer to run out. They sat waiting in the bedroom in complete silence.

The timer went off. Keren ran to the bathroom.

"And?" Olivia asked.

Keren stepped out of the bathroom, white as a ghost.

"We're fucked."

Chapter 10:

Ethan

"And now for our Valedictorian, Olivia Turner." Francois announced.

Ethan clapped, a small smile tugging on his face. Olivia walked onto the stage in her green graduation gown, a gold and white scarf draped over her shoulders.

She stepped up to the podium.

"Good morning, ladies and gentleman. It is my great honor and privilege to be this year's valedictorian."

Everyone in the audience seemed to hang onto her every word.

As Olivia spoke, Ethan realized he was enamored with the beautiful woman before him. He had missed her that morning when she went by his place to drop off her things.

Olivia's hair was curled into ringlets that made her look like a Hollywood starlet. Her lips were painted a cherry red, and her graduation cap sat perfectly on her head.

Everyone knew that Olivia was going to be Valedictorian. No one in the faculty was as dedicated and hard-working as she was.

The audience clapped, and Ethan snapped out of his daze, clapping along.

***

Ethan spotted Olivia out of the corner of his eye. She looked magnificent in the baby doll style powder blue dress that she was wearing. She was wearing white heels that made her long legs look even longer. She was sipping on a bottled water, laughing along with something one of the girls in her class was saying.

Ethan walked over to Olivia, smiling. She gave him a tight lipped smile in return.

Something was up.

"Congratulations on being Valedictorian." Ethan said. Olivia looked away, as if she was waiting for someone else to come over and talk to her.

"Thanks." Olivia said, not seemingly excited about her new found title.

"You also got the top grade in the bridge project." Ethan added.

Olivia hummed in response.

"The job at Knight Industries is yours." Ethan said.

Olivia hummed in response, still looking around.

Ethan stepped closer to Olivia, grabbing her chin to make her look at him.

"Okay, what's going on with you? You know how I feel about you not paying attention." Ethan spoke, his face a few inches away from Olivia's.

"Nothing. I'm just trying to mingle." Olivia remarked.

He could tell she was lying.

"That's not it. What happened?" Ethan asked.

Olivia tried to look away again, but Ethan turned her head back to him. He raised his eyebrows, waiting for her to respond.

Olivia rolled her eyes and tried to pull away from Ethan.

Ethan grabbed her wrist, and started dragging her away from the people.

Once outside of the building, he stopped. "Out with it."

Olivia crossed her arms over her waist. "I'm pregnant."

Ethan thought he had been punched in the face.

"What?"

Olivia looked like she wanted to cry.

"I...I don't know if I want to keep...*it*." Olivia said.

Ethan frowned.

"Why wouldn't you?"

Olivia stared at Ethan as if he was stupid. "Because why would I keep *it*?"

It bothered Ethan that Olivia was referring to the child as it.

"Because...it's our baby?" Ethan offered.

Olivia scoffed. "You married me so I could be a convenient fuck, and so that you could get a business deal."

Ethan was stunned. "But...it's still our baby."

Olivia rolled her eyes that were now tearing up. "So what, Ethan? Who cares?"

"I care."

Olivia scoffed. "Well, that doesn't matter."

"Why doesn't it matter?"

Olivia pinched the bridge of her nose. "Because...it just doesn't."

Ethan could tell there was more to this.

"Is this because you don't think you matter to me?"

Olivia sent a harsh glare. "Why the hell would that have anything to do with this?"

Ethan didn't know why he felt it may have had something to do with her decision.

"Look...this could just be me being selfish. But...I want to see if I can be a good dad. I never had one growing up, but I've seen how people with dads turn out. And...I want that. I will respect your decision, whatever you chose. You are my wife, after all. But if you can reconsider...I would like to give the whole family thing a shot."

Olivia tried to blink away her tears and awkwardly shuffled her feet.

"I'm scared, okay? My parents don't know you exist. They don't know we're married, and they don't know I'm pregnant. I don't know how to tell them. This...this isn't how I pictured my life going." Olivia managed to get out.

The tears now started flowing down her cheeks. She wiped them away angrily.

Ethan reached out for her, pulling her into a hug.

"We can figure this out." Ethan whispered into Olivia's hair.

He didn't know how, but for her, he'd make a way.

"How, Ethan? My parents aren't stupid. They'll do the math." Olivia sobbed.

"I don't know. But we can do this, together."

Ethan was uncertain of what he could do to ease Olivia's mind. All he knew, was that he wanted Olivia close to him, as is wife in more than just paperwork. He wanted her, wholly and completely. He wanted to have this baby with her. He wanted a family with her. He wanted to grow old with her.

"You're my all or nothing, Olivia Turner." Ethan whispered. "For you, I will do everything in my power to make you happy."

www.ingramcontent.com/pod-product-compliance
Lightning Source LLC
Chambersburg PA
CBHW061622130726
47996CB00003B/1083